THE GHOSTLY CAROUSEL

DELIGHTFULLY FRIGHTFUL POEMS

BY CALEF BROWN

Carolrhoda Books • Minneapolis

FOR CHARLES ADDAMS AND MERVYN PEAKE

Carolrhoda Books
A division of Lerner Publishing Group, Inc.
241 First Avenue North
Minneapolis, MN 55401 USA

For reading levels and more information, look up this title at
www.lernerbooks.com.

Designed by Kimberly Morales.
Main body text set in Imperfect OT 17/23. Typeface provided by T26.
The illustrations in this book were created with acrylic and gouache.

Library of Congress Cataloging-in-Publication Data

Names: Brown, Calef, author, illustrator.
Title: The ghostly carousel : delightfully frightful poems / Calef Brown.
Description: Minneapolis : Carolrhoda Books, 2018. | Audience: Ages 5–9. |
    Identifiers: LCCN 2017048406 (print) | LCCN 2017054836 (ebook) |
    ISBN 9781541524682 (eb pdf) | ISBN 9781512426618 (lb : acid-free paper)
Subjects: LCSH: Children's poetry, American.
Classification: LCC PS3552.R68525 (ebook) | LCC PS3552.R68525 A6 2018
    (print) | DDC 811/.54—dc23

LC record available at https://lccn.loc.gov/2017048406

Manufactured in the United States of America
1-41425-23336-1/3/2018

* CONTENTS *

COVEN TOTS

The children of the coven,
being far too young
to use the cauldron or the oven,
will often practice potions cold
with gazpacho as a base.
First they make a witchy face,
then add spiderwebs
and pumpkin guts,
cactus spines and hazelnuts.
Next they practice eerie chants,
which soon get boring.
Time to dance
around the mixture,
tossing crumbs
of hornet nests
and rotting plums
until the whole affair becomes
a horrid, stinky mess.
No magic is made,
but fun nonetheless!

JOEL

A zombie named Joel,
deep in a hole,
burrows
and furrows
his brow.
He needs to escape
from the family reunion
as quickly
as time
will allow.

His zombified aunts,
lost in a trance,
are lurching
and searching
for hugs.
"Your aunties are here!
With goodies!" they cheer.
"Scorpions,
leeches,
and slugs!"

GLUMM

The village of Glumm
is gloomy and grim
for miles in all directions.
A grisly, ghastly, ghostly place
except for these exceptions:
The dungeons, caves, and mausoleums
are fragrant, light, and airy,
and a day in the swamp
is a jubilant romp.
Everything else is scary.

THE GHOSTLY CAROUSEL

In last night's dream
I was all alone,
on my own
in a theme park.
Why, I thought,
did it seem so dark
in the early afternoon?
The air was filled with a haunting tune,
a single, lonely flügelhorn.
Suddenly—a unicorn!
A caribou,
a grizzly bear,
and a barracuda too,
all revolving slowly
on a ghostly carousel.
It had a crocodile as well.

THE JEKYLL LANTERN

"Carving a pumpkin is fun!"
Dr. Jekyll enthused.
But when it was done,
he was less than amused.
The face was infused
with a devilish aura
like something repugnant
released by Pandora.
An orangey fiend
with a horrid expression,
extremely ferocious
and full of aggression.
This terrible vision
he couldn't abide.
The doctor was helpless.
He had to go Hyde.

MEDUSA

Wicked Medusa—
she puts to good use a
team of hired help
to oil her scaly scalp
and comb the tangled snakes
with tongs and special rakes.
They do make mistakes
on a regular basis,
when someone, by chance,
takes a glance where her face is.

THE CREEPING CRUD

The Creeping
Creeping
Creeping
Crud—
a seeping flood
of noxious mud,
arriving precisely
at midnight on Fridays
complete with a stench
that will wrench your nose sideways
like a poisonous pie glaze,
oozing through sump pumps
and toppling floor lamps,
forming rug lumps,
and causing leg cramps
in neighborhoods
and summer camps
on balmy nights
when the world is sleeping . . .
The Crud is out there,
Creeping.

DUBLIN'S GOBLINS

Troubles abound
in Dublin town
every Halloween.
What will be found
if you wander around?
It's always the same routine:
trick-or-treating Leprechauns
causing a rowdy scene.
One of them gets an apple
or a moldy tangerine,
and this provokes
a slew of tricks.
Leprechauns are *mean*.

CANNIBAL Q & A

Q:

Why are cannibals
so fond of fondue?

A:

Dipping fingers in cheese
is so fun to do!

FRITZ

Undertaker Fritz
freely admits
to frequent fits of giggling
when a corpse burps
or a body starts wiggling.

CANARY CANOE

Wherever you travel,
whatever you do—
beware the canary canoe.
From out of the shadows
it floats into view.
Canaries seem harmless,
but this is untrue.
When songbirds are wronged
and prolonged in a cage,
they soon become quiet
and silently rage.
Plotting revenge
in elaborate ways,
they snatch a canoe
and escape in the haze.
Boaters and fisherman
answer their calls.
Suddenly—numerous
thunderous squalls!
No one is rescued.
There's nary a clue.
Beware the canary canoe.

HANK

A big, big fan
of the dark and dank.
That's Hank.
His favorite hangout
is a sunken bunker.
A deep thinker,
Hank the spelunker
is entranced by caves.
He rants and raves
about stalagmites, stalactites,
and powerful flashlights.
His world is dark and dank,
but his mood is always sunny.
Hank is a funny little dude.
He says that grubs and larvae
make *marvelous* food.

INSECT PIE (HANK'S RECIPE)

I like eating insect pie.
Want to know the reason why?
The reason is the cheese inside
the fleas inside the crust.
Tasty fleas are stuffed with cheese
until they nearly bust.
They're great with swiss
or, even better,
blended swirls
of jack and cheddar—
whatever kind that you can get.
You say you haven't tried it yet?
You absolutely must!
Enjoy the gooey cheese inside
the fleas inside the crust.

WARLOCKS

Telekinetic warlocks
can easily open door locks
of all different kinds
with their magical minds
using mighty brain jolts
known as "headvolts."
They even work on deadbolts.

WEE DEMON

To catch a wee demon
you simply have to trick it.
If you spy one in a gully
or a low-lying thicket,
distract it with a cricket bat
or a tennis racket,
then empty a sugar packet
into a stovepipe hat.

The wee demon
will tumble in,
just like that.

THE GAMBLING GHOST

The Gambling Ghost,
as everyone knows,
is not exactly nice.
He wails and moans.
He rolls the bones.
He never loses twice.
Ghouls and goblins
place their bets.
Then they pay the price.
The Gambling Ghost
is better than most
at using haunted dice.

SILHOUETTES

I'm not afraid
of bats or bee stings,
but late at night
I think I see things—
spooky silhouettes.
Look how wrinkled
my pillow gets,
gripped so very tightly.
Frozen with fright,
I ask the silhouettes politely
to please show themselves
as rows of toys
or clothes on shelves
in clever disguise.
Finally, then,
I can close my eyes.